MRS. O'LEARY'S COW

adapted by Mary Ann Hoberman

illustrated by Jenny Mattheson

LITTLE, BROWN AND COMPANY

New York ❧ Boston

Late one night
When we were all in bed,
Old Mother O'Leary
Left a lantern in the shed;
And when the cow kicked it over,
She winked her eye and said,

**"There'll be a hot time
In the old town tonight!"**

"Fire, Fire, Fire!"

The cow looked out
And started in to moo.
We got up
And wondered what to do;
And when the smoke poured out,
We started yelling, too,

"There'll be a hot time
In the old town tonight!"

Smoke!"

Smoke,

"Smoke,

The poor old cow
Was getting warm as toast.
The poor old cow,
She looked just like a ghost.
And as the flames crept near,
We feared that she would roast.

**"There'll be a hot time
In the old town tonight!"**

The fire truck
Came roaring down the street.
The fire spread. . . .
We all could feel the heat.
And as the siren blared,
We started to repeat,

"There'll be a hot time
In the old town tonight!"

"Water, Water, Water!"

The firefighters
Hooked the fire hose.
The water sprayed,
But still the fire rose.
And then we all cried out—
Now what do you suppose?—

*"There'll be a hot time
In the old town tonight!"*

"Ladder, Ladder, Ladder!"

They cranked it up
And they began to climb.
A wall collapsed. . . .
They did not have much time;
And as they neared the top,
We all began to chime,

*"There'll be a hot time
In the old town tonight!"*

"Save her,

Save her,

Save her!"

What a blaze!
Everyone was brave.
Up they climbed,
The poor old cow to save;
And when they brought her down,
We told her to behave,

*"You've made a hot time
In the old town tonight!"*

"Hooray, Hooray, Hooray!"

The firefighters
Put the fire out.
They rolled their hose
And shut the waterspout;
And as they drove away,
We all began to shout,

*"We've had a hot time
In the old town tonight!"*

"Thank you!

Thank you!

Thank you!"

Late that night
After she was fed,
We took the cow
And tucked her into bed;
And as she fell asleep,
She winked her eye and said,

*"I made a hot time
In the old town tonight!"*

"Moo, Moo, Moo!"

Also by Mary Ann Hoberman:

Bill Grogan's Goat

The Eensy-Weensy Spider

Mary Had a Little Lamb

Miss Mary Mack

You Read to Me, I'll Read to You

There Once Was a Man Named Michael Finnegan

Yankee Doodle

One of Each

The Looking Book

Fathers, Mothers, Sisters, Brothers

Also illustrated by Jenny Mattheson:

The Mouse, the Cat, and Grandmother's Hat

Christmas Morning

Happy to be Girls

The Great Tulip Trade

No Bows!

For my darling grandson, Ian. —M.A.H.

Text copyright © 2007 by Mary Ann Hoberman
Illustrations copyright © 2007 by Jenny Mattheson

Little, Brown and Company

Hachette Book Group USA
1271 Avenue of the Americas, New York, NY 10020
Visit our Web site at www.lb-kids.com

First Edition: April 2007

ISBN-13: 978-0-316-14840-5
ISBN-10: 0-316-14840-7

10 9 8 7 6 5 4 3 2 1

TWP

Printed in Singapore

Book design by Tracy Shaw

The illustrations for this book were done in oil paint on primed paper.
The text was set in Legacy Sans, and the display type is Adastra.